THE ODYSSEY

HOMER

Artist: Li Sidong

First edition for North America (including Canada and Mexico),
Philippine Islands, and Puerto Rico published in 2009
by Barron's Educational Series, Inc.

© The Salariya Book Company Limited 2009

All inquiries should be addressed to:
Barron's Educational Series, Inc.
250 Wireless Boulevard
Hauppauge, New York 11788
www.barronseduc.com

ISBN-13 (Hardcover): 978-0-7641-6243-5
ISBN-10 (Hardcover): 0-7641-6243-8
ISBN-13 (Paperback): 978-0-7641-4276-5
ISBN-10 (Paperback): 0-7641-4276-3

Library of Congress Control No.: 2008939081

Picture credits:
p. 40: AAAC/TopFoto.co.uk
p. 45: Topham Picturepoint/TopFoto.co.uk
Every effort has been made to trace copyright holders. The Salariya Book Company apologizes for any
omissions and would be pleased, in such cases, to add an acknowledgment in future editions.

Date of Manufacture: July 2013
Manufactured by: Hong Kong Graphics, Shanghai, China

Printed and bound in China
9 8 7 6 5 4 3 2

THE ODYSSEY

HOMER

Illustrated by

Li Sidong

BARRON'S

Retold by

Fiona Macdonald

Series created and designed by

David Salariya

THE HERO of our story is Odysseus, who destroyed the mighty city of Troy by the trick of the wooden horse. On his way home he visited many countries and suffered many hardships. Poseidon, god of the sea, tried to prevent him from ever reaching home—but Odysseus would never give up.

I, HOMER, pray to the goddess of poetry to help me tell his story.

CHARACTERS*

Odysseus, prince
(later king) of Ithaca

Penelope, his wife

Telemachus, their son

Menelaus, king of Sparta

Agamemnon, high king
of the Greeks

Calypso, a goddess

Helen, wife of Menelaus
and lover of Paris

Paris, a prince of Troy

Circe, an enchantress

Aphrodite, goddess of
love

Athena, goddess of
wisdom and of war

Poseidon, god of the sea

Zeus, king
of the gods

Homer,
the greatest
Greek poet

*See page 41 for a guide to pronouncing the Greek names.

INTRODUCING ODYSSEUS

This is the story of the ancient Greek hero Odysseus. Centuries ago, I, Homer, told of his adventures in my famous poems, the *Iliad* and the *Odyssey*.

Odysseus is born on the Greek island of Ithaca,* where his father is king. As a child, Odysseus is badly hurt while hunting wild boar in the woods.

The scar on his thigh never fades.

Good shot!

As a young man, Odysseus sails to Messenia on the Greek mainland.

The son of Messenia's king gives him a wonderful bow. It's so powerful that only Odysseus can string it.[1]

Odysseus grows up tough and strong—a natural leader, admired by everyone. He's clever, energetic, brave—and sometimes disobedient and headstrong.

He's very intelligent!

He's not especially handsome, but he's friendly and interesting, with an entertaining way of talking.

A king's son must marry. It's time for Odysseus to find a wife. He sets off for the kingdom of Sparta, home of Princess Helen.

Who wouldn't want to marry Helen?

* For places mentioned in the story, see the map on pages 42–43.
1. only Odysseus can string it: The bow is so stiff that it's almost impossible to bend it so that the bowstring can be looped over the ends of the bow.

TWO WEDDINGS

Helen is no ordinary mortal. Her father is Zeus, mighty king of the gods. Her mother is Leda, a queen who fell in love with Zeus when he transformed himself into a swan. They say that Helen was hatched from a giant egg!

Now she's considered the most beautiful woman in the world.

She's moving grace—a ray of golden light!

The king of Sparta is looking for a husband for Helen.

He's invited all the Greek princes to his court.

He chooses Menelaus, a rich and powerful prince from Mycenae.

Odysseus and all the other princes swear lifelong loyalty to Menelaus.

Odysseus is still determined to find a wife for himself.

One whose heart and ways are kind...

He makes an excellent choice.

The lovely Penelope is wise, gracious, gentle, and loving. Her devoted family can hardly bear to let her go.

To rocky Ithaca!

The newly married couple leave for home, with hearts full of hope.

Menelaus is now king of Sparta.

He and Helen are happy together—but not for long…

Aphrodite, goddess of love, is about to meddle with their lives.

She has a favorite among men: the handsome Paris, prince of Troy.[1]

Three powerful goddesses[2] have asked Paris to judge which of them is the most beautiful.

Hera

Athena

Aphrodite

I give the prize to Aphrodite!

Paris travels to Sparta.

Aphrodite has bribed Paris by promising to make Helen fall in love with him. The other goddesses are furious, and plot revenge.

King Menelaus welcomes Paris and entertains him royally.

Aphrodite sends Menelaus away on an urgent mission.

Left alone, Paris and Helen fall passionately in love—just as Aphrodite promised!

Paris is as handsome as a god!

Helen's a goddess among women!

They run away together to Troy.

Menelaus is furious.

He calls on his brother Agamemnon—great warrior, great king—and all the Greek princes to go to war against Troy.

---

1. Troy: a splendid city and kingdom in Asia Minor (present-day Turkey).
2. Three powerful goddesses: Hera, wife of Zeus; Athena, goddess of wisdom and of warfare; Aphrodite, goddess of love.

THE MADNESS OF ODYSSEUS

Meanwhile, Odysseus and Penelope live very happily on the island of Ithaca.

Where can a man find greater joy than in his own home with his own family?

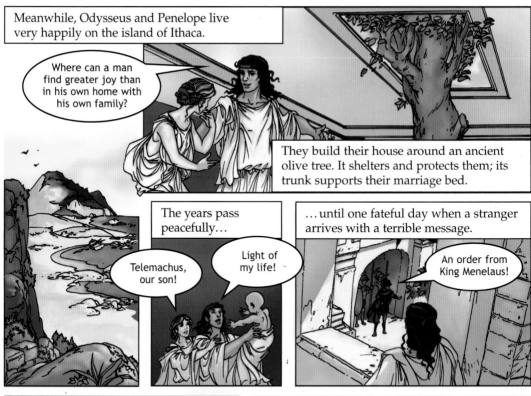

They build their house around an ancient olive tree. It shelters and protects them; its trunk supports their marriage bed.

The years pass peacefully…

Telemachus, our son!

Light of my life!

…until one fateful day when a stranger arrives with a terrible message.

An order from King Menelaus!

It's war against Troy! Odysseus must keep his promise to support Menelaus.

Penelope! My own land! My people!

The thought of leaving home breaks his heart.

When will he return? The palace seer[1] foretells a grim future.

After nineteen years—and all your shipmates will be lost!

Odysseus pretends to be mad to escape his duty. He tries to plow with an ox and a donkey.

Hmm!

Of course, the two animals won't work together.

The messenger is suspicious. He catches sight of Odysseus's baby son.

Aha!

1. seer: a wise man or magician who can foretell the future.

He snatches Telemachus and throws him in front of the plow!

Waaah!

Odysseus dashes to the rescue…

Telemachus!

…and proves that he is not mad after all!

It's no use playing tricks! Odysseus must do his duty. He must leave home and fight in the war.

Odysseus sails away to join the great army.

So Menelaus is determined to get his revenge!

Together, Odysseus and Menelaus go to find Paris. They try to arrange peace.

But there can be no peace—the goddesses Hera and Athena are still angry with Paris, and want Menelaus to punish him.

The Greeks arrive off the coast of Troy…

…while goddess Aphrodite weaves magic spells to keep Paris madly in love with Helen.

Who can blame the Trojans[1] and the Greeks for fighting over such a woman?

1. Trojans: people of Troy.

THE TROJAN WAR

The Trojan War will last for nine long years.

Many brave men on both sides are destined to die: Achilles, Hector, Ajax—even handsome Paris, Helen's lover.

Achilles

Ajax

Hector

Athena and Hera fill the Greeks with hatred of the Trojans.

Aphrodite takes the Trojans' side.

Odysseus is Athena's favorite.

Save the Greeks from disaster!

With her help, he persuades the young hero Achilles to join in the fight.

Helped by Athena, Odysseus cures the wounded King Telephus. In return, Telephus shows the Greeks the quickest way to Troy.

There is Priam's[1] high city.

Odysseus kills seven men in one fight. He steals wonderful warhorses from the king of Thrace.[2]

Help us, goddess! Hurry! Get the horses away!

---

1. Priam: the elderly king of Troy, and father of Paris.
2. Thrace: a country which included parts of present-day Bulgaria, Turkey, Greece, Serbia, and Macedonia.

In a nighttime raid, he captures a dangerous Trojan spy.

Answer my questions!

Don't kill me! I'll pay a ransom![1]

When the Greek hero Achilles is killed by Paris, Odysseus carries back the body from the battlefield.

He was godlike and glorious!

He captures a Trojan seer and makes him reveal crucial secrets.

Fetch the holy bones of Pelops![2]

Summon Philoctectes![3]

Steal the Palladium[4] from Troy's great temple!

Last of all, Athena sends Odysseus a brilliant idea:

It's a trick!

It's a gift of thanks to Athena!

The Greeks must make a huge, hollow wooden horse.

Thinking that the horse might please the angry goddess Athena, the Trojans drag it into their city.

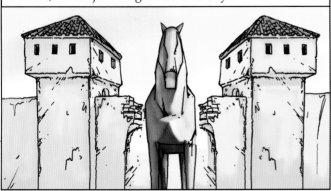

But during the night, twelve of the best Greek warriors leap out of the horse! They fling open Troy's gates and the Greek army rushes in. Troy is destroyed, and all its people slaughtered or captured as slaves.

And all by Athena's power!

1. ransom: money paid for the release of a prisoner. This was a normal part of warfare in ancient and medieval times.
2. Pelops: a dead hero, and ancestor of many famous warriors.
3. Philoctetes: a fierce fighter who guards the deadly bow and arrows belonging to the superhuman Heracles (Hercules).
4. Palladium: a sacred robe with magic, protective powers.

Homeward Bound

The long war is over. Odysseus is older, wiser, sadder. Now, more than anything else in the world, he wants to go home to Ithaca, to Penelope and Telemachus.

Ithaca! There is nowhere on earth I love better!

Odysseus has been away for ten terrible years.

Home and family! How I long to see them!

Westward, away from Troy!

He sets sail with a fleet of twelve ships.

The winds blow them to a city on the coast of Thrace.

It's the home of our enemies, the Ciconians!

Odysseus defeats the Ciconians. Only one priest, Maron, survives.

In return for sparing his life, Maron gives them some rare magic wine.

The sailors feast greedily…

…ignoring Odysseus when he orders them to leave.

Too late! The Ciconian army arrives.

Six seats are empty in each ship!

Seventy-two of Odysseus's men are killed. The rest just manage to escape.

Zeus, king of the gods, is angry with Odysseus's men for attacking the Ciconians. He sends a terrible storm.

We face death in this raging sea!

After nine days drifting out of control, they reach the coast of Libya, in north Africa.

Odysseus sends scouts ashore.

Fresh water!

Fruit and flowers!

Surely it's safe to rest awhile in this beautiful place?

The people seem harmless.

But this is the land of the Lotus-Eaters. If they eat the magic lotus flowers, they'll forget everything—even who they are!

The scouts eat the flowers and stagger back to the beach, confused and forgetful. They call for the other sailors to join them. Lazy, hazy lotus-eating is delightful!

Woo-hoo!

Come and try it!

Only the wise Odysseus realizes the danger. He orders them back on board, but the scouts aren't listening.

In the Cave of the Cyclops

Dazed by lotus, Odysseus and his men could be trapped here for ever! He orders the scouts to be dragged back to the ships, kicking and protesting.

Clear the beach! Don't let anyone else eat lotus, or we'll lose all hope of home!

More! I want more!

They sail away, and reach a cluster of islands.

It's a wilderness!

The biggest island is home to the Cyclopes![1] But Odysseus doesn't know this yet. He's just pleased to have found a good harbor.

Grunt!

Some god has guided us!

Odysseus's ship anchors in a calm, sheltered bay.

The Cyclopes keep flocks of sheep on the island's green pastures. But they have no laws, no fields, no ships, no communities.

They're savages!

1. Cyclopes (pronounced "SY-clo-pees"): a race of brutal giants with one eye in the middle of their foreheads. "Cyclopes" is the plural of "Cyclops," which means "round eye" in Greek.

Next morning, Odysseus sails across to the Cyclopes' island. Twelve sailors go with him.

We'll find out who this island belongs to.

A sheepfold[1] and a cave!

The cave is full of rich, creamy cheeses, all freshly made.

Baaa!

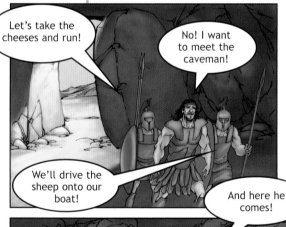

Let's take the cheeses and run!

No! I want to meet the caveman!

We'll drive the sheep onto our boat!

And here he comes!

STOMP... STOMP!

Strangers!

A huge boulder blocks the entrance to the cave. Odysseus and the surviving sailors are trapped!

1. sheepfold: a pen for sheep or goats.

17

NOBODY

The beastly Cyclops eats two sailors for breakfast, and two more for his supper. While he sleeps off his grisly meal, cunning Odysseus thinks up a plan.

Try some of our wine!

Thank you!

BURP!

What's your name?

Odysseus gives the gorged[1] monster some of Maron's magic wine.[2] He waits till the Cyclops is completely drunk before answering his question.

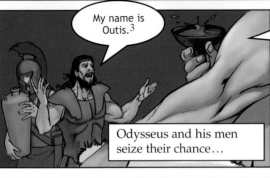

My name is Outis.[3]

AAARGH!

They blind the drunken Cyclops with a pointed stick.

Odysseus and his men seize their chance…

In agony, the monster cries out to the other Cyclopes for help. But, taken in by Odysseus's false name, they ignore him.

What's the matter, Polyphemus?

Nobody's tricked me! Nobody's wounded me!

You fooled them!

But we still have to find a way out of here!

The blind Cyclops staggers around the cave.

But the men still can't escape. The Cyclops would surely feel or hear them if they tried to tiptoe past him.

The next morning, the Cyclops rolls the boulder away from the cave entrance.

Ugh! The pain!

How can we get away?

1. gorged: greedily stuffed full of food.
2. Maron's magic wine: see page 14.
3. Outis: Greek for "nobody."

Wily Odysseus has another clever idea. The Cyclops's sheep are huge and strong, with long, curly fleeces.

Baaa! Baaa!

A man could hide underneath one and never be found!

The Cyclops pats his sheep as they leave the cave—but he does not find Odysseus and his men tied underneath them.

Oh sheep, if only you could tell me where Nobody is hiding!

Free at last, Odysseus and the surviving sailors dash for their ship.

Hurry up!

Safely back on board, Odysseus jeers at the Cyclops.

You shouldn't eat your visitors!

Zeus and the gods have punished you with blindness!

Be careful, sir! You'll only provoke him.

He'll smash our ship!

The furious Cyclops hurls a huge boulder at the ship…

…but, luckily, the splash just pushes the ship further on.

So Odysseus and his men think they are safe, but worse is to come…

19

Aeolus and the Winds

As the Cyclops gets ready to hurl another massive rock, Odysseus continues to taunt him.

I, Odysseus, destroyer of cities, blinded you!

Hear me, Lord Poseidon!

I hear!

Deep beneath the waves, Poseidon, god of the sea, hears the wounded Cyclops's prayer.

Angry Poseidon decrees a cruel fate for Odysseus and his sailors. It will be many years before Odysseus reaches home—and all his companions will die on the journey.

They sail on through stormy seas.

Now even more of my friends are dead.

Land ahoy!

At last they sight a strange floating island.

As they draw near, they see a royal palace with walls of shining bronze.

It belongs to Aeolus…

Welcome to my home.

…guardian of the winds.

They are guests in his palace for a month. They rest, they feast, they play sports, and they tell tales of their epic adventures.

When it's time to leave, Aeolus gives Odysseus a magnificent present. It's a leather bag…

…with all the wild winds tied up inside it!

As long as the bag stays closed, Odysseus need never worry that the winds will be against him.

Aeolus stirs just a gentle breeze to blow them back to Ithaca.

Full of hope, Odysseus and his men sail on for nine days and nine nights.

Look! The coast of Ithaca!

At last I'll see Penelope again!

I can see people on the shore, lighting fires and cooking.

But, exhausted from steering the ship, Odysseus falls asleep.

What's in the bag?

Zzzzzz! Zzzzz!

It must be treasure!

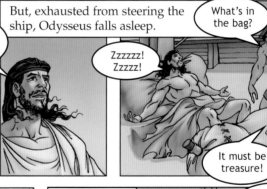

What about our share? Almost home, with no gold or silver?

Open it!

WHOOOSH!

A screaming hurricane blasts the ship back to Aeolus's island.

Where is Ithaca now?

Go! I will not help a man cursed by the gods!

Aeolus is angry and will not help them again.

Giants—and Sorcery

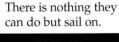
There is nothing they can do but sail on.

After six days, they spy a pleasant-looking island with a fine harbor, sheltered by high cliffs. But there's something strange about it…

In this land, dawn follows dusk. There's no night!

There's no comfort for us!

Three scouts swim ashore. They meet a very tall girl. Without speaking, she points the way to her father's house.

What people live here? Where is their leader?

The people here are giants—and they're hungry!

One helpless scout is torn in two and devoured. The other scouts run for their lives.

The whole tribe of giants chases after them, baying for blood.

They pelt the ships with rocks and spear the helpless sailors like fish.

Only Odysseus's own ship, anchored further from the shore, escapes the butchery.

Row, men, row! Row till your hearts burst!

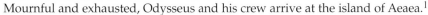

Mournful and exhausted, Odysseus and his crew arrive at the island of Aeaea.[1]

More grief!

It's enchanting—and enchanted!

This time the frightened men draw lots to decide who goes ashore.

We'll stay close to the shore.

A fine house stands half-hidden in the trees.

Welcome! I am Circe.

A beautiful woman greets the men. Lions and wolves prowl around, wagging their tails in a friendly way—most strange!

One of the men wisely decides to wait outside.

Is she a goddess? Or a witch?

The rest go in with Circe, who graciously offers them food and wine. It's all delicious—but as they eat, they find themselves changing shape…

Oink!

Grunt!

…and Circe drives them all into a pigsty!

The lone watchman rushes back to find Odysseus.

They've been transformed by evil magic!

Suddenly a dazzling figure appears before Odysseus.

Odysseus, beware!

It's Hermes, messenger of the gods!

1. Aeaea: pronounced "eye-EYE-a."

A VISIT TO THE DEAD

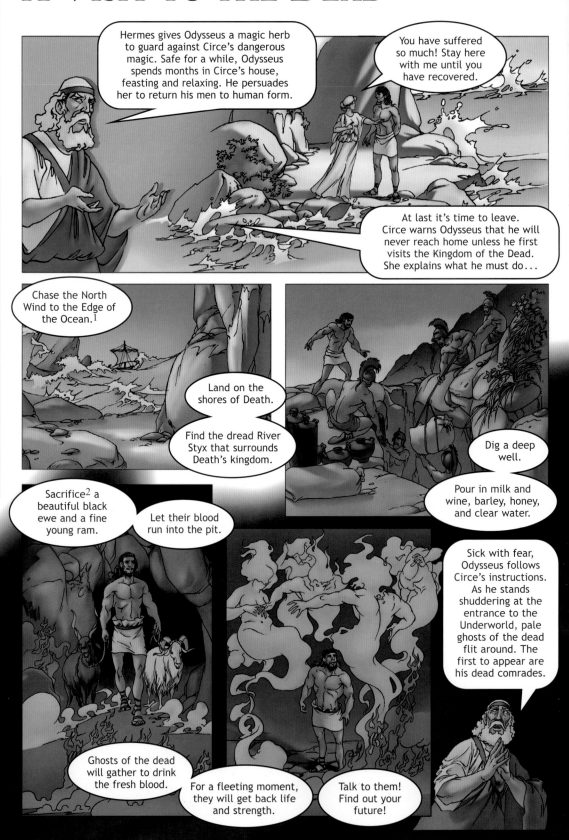

Hermes gives Odysseus a magic herb to guard against Circe's dangerous magic. Safe for a while, Odysseus spends months in Circe's house, feasting and relaxing. He persuades her to return his men to human form.

You have suffered so much! Stay here with me until you have recovered.

At last it's time to leave. Circe warns Odysseus that he will never reach home unless he first visits the Kingdom of the Dead. She explains what he must do...

Chase the North Wind to the Edge of the Ocean.[1]

Land on the shores of Death.

Find the dread River Styx that surrounds Death's kingdom.

Dig a deep well.

Pour in milk and wine, barley, honey, and clear water.

Sacrifice[2] a beautiful black ewe and a fine young ram.

Let their blood run into the pit.

Sick with fear, Odysseus follows Circe's instructions. As he stands shuddering at the entrance to the Underworld, pale ghosts of the dead flit around. The first to appear are his dead comrades.

Ghosts of the dead will gather to drink the fresh blood.

For a fleeting moment, they will get back life and strength.

Talk to them! Find out your future!

1. Ocean: the ancient Greeks believed that the Ocean was a huge river that surrounded the world.
2. Sacrifice: kill as an offering to the gods or spirits.

Next, Odysseus sees the spirit of Tiresias, a famous Greek seer. Tiresias lived for seven generations—in both male and female bodies! He drinks the blood, then speaks:

Odysseus, man of woe! Poseidon is still angry with you.

Sorrow and suffering lie ahead.

You WILL reach home one day—

—so long as you don't harm the holy cattle on the Sun God's island.

But do not despair!

There's more trouble waiting for you at home.

But be brave. Go on another long journey to sacrifice to the gods.

I must leave home again?

Then, only then, will you be able to live in peace.

Tiresias vanishes, and a pale, sad crowd of ghosts gather 'round—dead heroes hopelessly longing to taste life once more.

Odysseus tries to hug his mother's ghost, but she slips through his fingers.

I died of grief when you did not come home.

The ghosts swoop and swirl around Odysseus. So many! Such sad fates!

He meets the glorious King Agamemnon.

Learn from me! Don't trust anyone. I was betrayed and murdered.[1]

Horror overwhelms him. Shaking, sickened, he races back to his ship.

1. betrayed and murdered: When he returned home from the Trojan War, Agamemnon was murdered by his wife Clytemnestra and her lover Aegisthus.

Perils at Sea

Odysseus returns to Circe's island one last time. Then it's time to set sail for the unknown again.

Circe has warned Odysseus of the dangers he has to face.

Hard times lie ahead, Odysseus, beween you and your homecoming, old and alone.

Beware of the Sirens, half woman, half bird.

Their beautiful singing lures men to their death on the treacherous rocks.

You must plug your crew's ears with wax, so they don't hear the Sirens' song.

If you want to listen to the Sirens, get your men to tie you to the mast—

—then you won't be tempted to steer the ship towards the danger.

The Sirens' lovely music drifts across the waves.

Come to us, glorious Greeks!

Their singing is like dreams, like pearls, like honey!

Noble Odysseus, come to us!

Untie me!

We know of your bravery.

We know the future.

The sailors refuse to set Odysseus free until the ship has sailed out of danger.

Rest on your oars, my faithful crew!

Odysseus has heard the Sirens' song and lived!

Fresh dangers lie ahead.

Zeus help us!

On one side, six-headed, serpent-necked Scylla lies in wait to snatch travellers in her jaws. Her bloody fangs are sharp as daggers.

Facing her is the roaring whirlpool Charybdis.

She greedily gulps down sea water, sucking sailors to their deaths at the bottom of the sea.

They must pass between jagged rocks and sheer cliffs.

Odysseus must steer a course between these two mortal dangers.

Following Circe's advice, he makes an offering to Hecate, goddess of the Underworld.

Where's this monster? Let me fight!

He prepares to do battle…

… but it's hopeless.

Six of his sailors fall victim to Scylla's six heads.

THE CATTLE OF THE SUN GOD

With heavy hearts, the survivors sail on. Troubled and travel-weary, they reach the island of the Sun God.

Odysseus remembers the warning from Tiresias.

You must not harm the cattle on the Sun God's island!

He would prefer to sail straight past—but the men are exhausted.

You must all promise not to touch the cattle.

We swear.

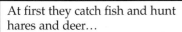

They land on the island—and Poseidon sends a furious storm to stop them from sailing away.

At first they catch fish and hunt hares and deer…

…but they gaze longingly at the fine fat cattle grazing peacefully in the meadows!

Wise goddess Athena, help me!

One day, while Odysseus is saying his prayers, the temptation is just too much for them…

What have you done?

We will all suffer for this!

They have committed a crime against the gods—and the gods see everything!

Sure enough, Helios, the Sun God, complains to mighty Zeus.

I want revenge!

I will stop shining and plunge the world into darkness!

Zeus persuades Helios to go on shining…

Odysseus must be punished—and his crew!

…but he, too, is angry about the cattle.

Odysseus could stay on the island and wait for the gods' punishment…

I am desperate to get home!

…but instead he bravely decides to set sail…

Six days we've travelled, far out to sea.

…and risk whatever the gods may send him.

Then, with wild winds and terrifying thunder, their punishment arrives!

I'll make splinters of their ship!

Zeus sends a terrific storm. Odysseus's ship is smashed and all the crewmen—eaters of fobidden meat—are drowned.

Only Odysseus survives, surrounded by shattered timbers.

Weak and exhausted, he clings to the wreckage.

But a vicious wind, sent by Zeus, blows him toward an even greater danger…

The whirlpool Charybdis!

CALYPSO AND NAUSICAA

But Charybdis spits out Odysseus and the remains of his ship.

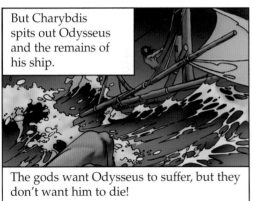

The gods want Odysseus to suffer, but they don't want him to die!

Odysseus drifts for days, and then he is washed ashore on a blissful island. Calypso, goddess of lovely songs, lives here, surrounded by birds and trees, flowers and waterfalls. It's a paradise!

Calypso falls in love with Odysseus. She promises he will live forever, as long as he stays on her island.

Beloved guest!

Divine Calypso!

They even begin a family.

We have two fine sons!

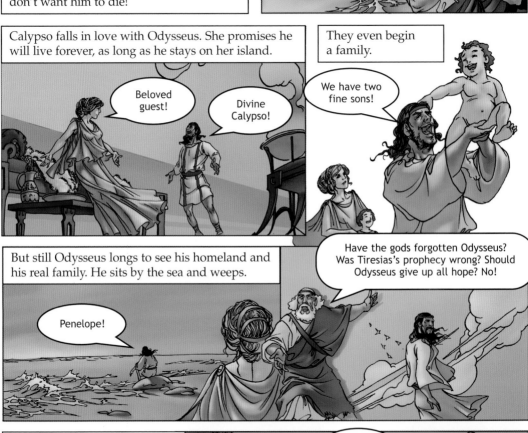

But still Odysseus longs to see his homeland and his real family. He sits by the sea and weeps.

Penelope!

Have the gods forgotten Odysseus? Was Tiresias's prophecy wrong? Should Odysseus give up all hope? No!

Goddess Athena persuades Zeus, king of the gods, to let Odysseus leave Calypso's island. Calypso is heartbroken —but Zeus must be obeyed. She gives Odysseus wood to make a boat, and food and water for his journey. She calls up a kindly wind to speed him on his way.

Farewell, my love!

Odysseus speeds on, steering a straight course by the stars. His heart is full of joy. But his bitter enemy, Poseidon, is watching him.

He's nearly home—but I'll give him a rough ride!

He swims for two days until he reaches an island. Exhausted, he crawls ashore.

Angry Poseidon whips up another furious storm.

Odysseus is saved from drowning by a sea nymph[1] who cradles him in her shawl.

CRASH!

I can hear girls laughing!

Odysseus has lost all his clothes in the shipwreck, so he hides behind some bushes.

Odysseus is a wretched sight—wild-eyed, salt-stained, and grimy. The girls run away—all except one.

She is Princess Nausicaa, the lovely daughter of the king of this island.

Gracious lady, are you a girl or a goddess?

Eek!

Good sir, are you a castaway[2]?

We must take care of you!

She finds clothes for him and leads him to the palace.

Friend, come and share our feast!

To Ithaca — at last!

Odysseus entertains the king and queen with the story of his adventures.

When it's time to leave, they give him a magic ship.

It will take him home, all by itself!

1. nymph: a minor goddess or nature-spirit in the shape of a beautiful young woman.
2. castaway: one who washes ashore after having survived a shipwreck.

ITHACA

Odysseus climbs on board, and falls into a deep, dreamless sleep. He is still sleeping when the ship reaches Ithaca. The gods be praised! He's home again after almost 20 years!

But his troubles are not over...

A thick mist covers the island, and Odysseus feels lost. A tall, stately woman approaches...

Where am I?

I am always watching over you, to help and protect you. Now, listen to me!

It's the goddess Athena, here in Odysseus's homeland!

For three long years, greedy suitors[1] have been trying to wed your wife Penelope.

They want her beauty—and your kingdom!

You will need all your cleverness to get rid of them, and save her.

Athena tells Odysseus what has been happening in Ithaca.

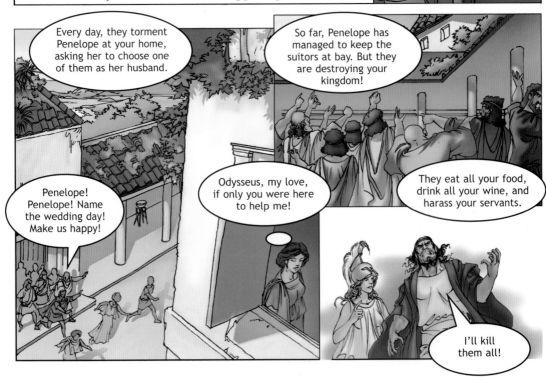

Every day, they torment Penelope at your home, asking her to choose one of them as her husband.

So far, Penelope has managed to keep the suitors at bay. But they are destroying your kingdom!

Penelope! Penelope! Name the wedding day! Make us happy!

Odysseus, my love, if only you were here to help me!

They eat all your food, drink all your wine, and harass your servants.

I'll kill them all!

1. suitors: men who want to marry. Because Odysseus has been away so long, most people assume that he is dead, and that Penelope is a widow.

Athena disguises Odysseus as a poor wandering beggar. That way, he can spy on the suitors without being recognized. Then she leaves Ithaca and speeds off to Sparta to fetch Telemachus, Odysseus's son.

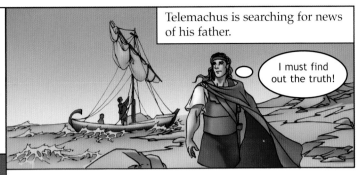

Telemachus is searching for news of his father.

I must find out the truth!

Odysseus finds shelter with his faithful swineherd.[1]

Welcome, stranger!

The old man does not recognize him, but is kind and friendly.

They talk about the good times long ago…

He went to fight overseas—a great loss to the kingdom.

…when Odysseus lived and ruled in Ithaca!

Magically, Telemachus appears, brought from Sparta by Athena.

While the swineherd is out feeding his pigs, Odysseus tells Telemachus who he is. Father and son hug each other joyfully.

Look who's here!

Father—we thought you were dead!

Home at last, my boy!

Next morning, on the way to the palace, Odysseus and Telemachus pass a very old dog by the side of the road. It's Argos, Odysseus's faithful hound. He recognizes his master, wags his tail—and dies of happiness.

In just a few minutes, I'll see my darling Penelope!

1. swineherd: a farmworker who looks after pigs.

PENELOPE AND THE SUITORS

At the palace, the greedy suitors are feasting, boasting, quarrelling.

More, you fool!

Cheers!

Delicious!

Odysseus controls his anger and watches them carefully, planning how to attack.

Most of them ignore Odysseus, but one beats and insults him.

I'll deal with him later!

He recognizes Penelope. She's older, of course, but still lovely.

That's her! My dear, dear wife!

Odysseus's heart leaps with joy, but he stays silent.

Penelope speaks to the suitors.

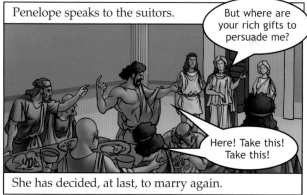

But where are your rich gifts to persuade me?

Here! Take this! Take this!

She has decided, at last, to marry again.

Odysseus breathes a sigh of relief: Penelope has not yet married!

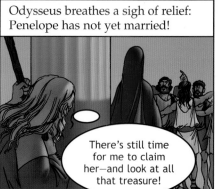

There's still time for me to claim her—and look at all that treasure!

Night falls. Odysseus and Telemachus clear the hall.

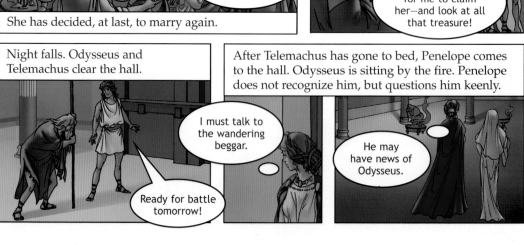

I must talk to the wandering beggar.

Ready for battle tomorrow!

After Telemachus has gone to bed, Penelope comes to the hall. Odysseus is sitting by the fire. Penelope does not recognize him, but questions him keenly.

He may have news of Odysseus.

They talk. Penelope tells the "beggar" of the clever trick she has played on the suitors. She has asked them to wait until she has finished weaving a shroud[1] for Odysseus's father. Each night she unravels[2] all she has woven during the day, so the shroud is never finished. But now her trick has been discovered!

Oh, how I long for Odysseus!

Now I must marry one of the suitors, or else they will ruin the kingdom!

Believe me, Madam...

...one day soon, Odysseus will return to your loving arms—and he'll bring peace to Ithaca!

Thank you for those kind words. Now my servant will wash your tired, dusty feet and make a bed for you by the fire.

As the old servant washes his feet, she sees the scar on his thigh, made when the wild boar wounded him![3]

Master! Is it really you?

Silence! No one must know!

The goddess Athena has told Penelope to hold a shooting match for the suitors...

They must shoot with Odysseus's great bow.[4]

...and marry the winner!

Good night, beggar! I go to sleep on my lonely bed, and weep for my long-lost Odysseus.

1. shroud: a fine cloth for wrapping a dead body.
2. unravels: undoes the weaving.
3. when the wild boar wounded him: see page 7.
4. Odysseus's great bow: see page 7.

THE BOW OF ODYSSEUS

At a great feast the next day, the shooting match is announced.

Here is Odysseus's great bow!

We're ready!

These axes will be your target.

Puff! Phew!

None of us is strong enough to use it!

Odysseus brings the faithful swineherd and his sons.

Strangely, the goddess Athena commands me to ask the beggar!

Wandering beggar, will you try the bow?

Telemachus sends the women away. Then the doors are bolted. There will be no escape!

Mother! Women servants! Please leave the hall!

My bow sings! It knows its rightful owner!

Odysseus picks up the mighty bow as if it were a feather, and bends it easily!

CRASH!

Zeus sends a mighty peal of thunder as Odysseus takes aim…

...and shoots a single arrow straight through all the axes!

Let's get out of here!

Gasp! Is he a man or a god?

He casts off his disguise...

Die, you dogs! This is my revenge!

...and the battle begins.

Quick! Get your weapons! We'll overpower him!

Telemachus and the swineherd's sons join in.

Either fight your way out...

...or run away like cowards!

Odysseus pardons a musician who had played for the suitors...

I'll call the servants to clear away the bodies.

...but everyone else is killed.

Odysseus purifies the hall with prayers and incense.[1]

1. incense: herbs, resins, and spices, burned to give off sweet-smelling smoke.

HAPPY AT LAST

At last the time has come for Odysseus to be reunited with his faithful Penelope. He has faced many dangers, and found love and friendship. But he has never forgotten his homeland or his family. Now his loyalty is rewarded.

Penelope enters the palace hall. The old servant woman has told her that Odysseus is waiting there.

My heart is in a whirl!

She is doubtful, frightened...

He is just like Odysseus—but is this a trick? I'll test him!

Stranger, you may stay a while.

Servant, go and get Odysseus's old bed ready. It's in a spare room upstairs.

My bed? Moved to a spare room? Lady, that's impossible! I built that bed myself, around a living olive tree. No other man has ever seen it! It's our secret!

At last, Penelope believes him.

Dear, dear, wife!

Dear husband, do not be angry!

They say he has grown old and weak.

The next day, Odysseus goes to visit his elderly father.

I thought I would die, and never see you again!

But a new danger threatens: the dead suitors' families and friends!

Where is Odysseus! We want revenge!

Odysseus and his father fight back...

We're outnumbered!

Even with the help of the swineherd and other servants, they are soon surrounded. Is Odysseus's joyful homecoming doomed to end in disaster? No!

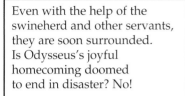

PUT DOWN YOUR WEAPONS! I, goddess Athena, command you! Do not dare to disobey! No one shall fight on this island!

Odysseus's life is saved! But this is not quite the end of his adventures.

He still needs to make peace with the angry god Poseidon. To do this, he must cross the storm-tossed sea and travel far inland.

There he must sacrifice a bull, a boar, and a ram.

But the gods are just. In return, Poseidon will send a blessing. Odysseus will sail home to a life of love, peace, and plenty—and his death will be gentle.

THE END

HOMER (8th century B.C. or thereabouts)

Homer is one of the most famous writers in the world. His poetry has been praised for over 2,000 years. Yet we know very little about him, and some scholars claim that he never even existed!

Homer's name is first recorded sometime around 800 B.C. to 750 B.C. This was the era when a new Greek alphabet had just been invented, and Greek poems and songs were being written down for the first time. For centuries before then, Greek poems had been memorized and passed on by word of mouth. Some poets and musicians (these poems were often sung to music) lived in royal palaces as honored servants of kings and great warriors; others wandered from village to village, entertaining anyone who would pay them or give them food and shelter.

Imaginary portrait of Homer: a Roman copy of a classical Greek statue

WHO WROTE HOMER'S POEMS?

Experts in ancient languages think that many passages in Homer's poems were memorized and passed on in this way. Archeologists say that they were probably composed between about 1200 and 1100 B.C., because they contain descriptions of bronze weapons and armor that were used by the Greeks at that time, but not in later centuries.

Because of this evidence, some scholars think that "Homer" was an invented name given to a whole group of earlier poets whose names had been forgotten, at the time when the poems were first written down around 800–750 B.C. But most scholars think that there was a real poet called Homer, who used fragments of much older poems to create his own new masterpieces and get them written down, also around 800–750 B.C.

WAS THERE A REAL HOMER?

The ancient Greeks who lived from around 600 B.C. onward certainly believed that a poet called Homer had once lived. They claimed that he was born either in Asia Minor (now Turkey) or on the eastern Greek island of Chios. They also thought that he was blind. This may be because they misunderstood his name ("Homer" sounds rather like a Greek word that means "without sight"), but it may have been true. Being a poet was one of the few ways in which blind people in ancient Greece could earn a living.

The ancient Greeks honored Homer as one of their nation's great people. His works were said to be "the best Greek ever written," and were used as models for lesser poets to copy. Around 200 B.C., ancient Greek scholars working in Egypt copied out a complete collection of Homer's important poems—and included some other works which were probably not by him. After Greek power collapsed, these texts disappeared for centuries, until they were discovered and preserved by Muslim scholars. From Egypt, they passed to medieval Europe, reaching Italy in 1354. The first printed version of Homer's poems was published in Italy in 1488.

TWO GREAT POEMS

Today, Homer is remembered and admired for two great epics. (Epics are long poems about the adventures of great heroes.) The *Iliad* tells a tragic story of love and war, centered on the siege of the splendid city of Troy and featuring many mighty heroes. The *Odyssey* describes the adventures of one Greek warrior, Odysseus, as he tries to return home from fighting in the Trojan War. His crewmen anger the gods, and so he has to endure many dangers and overcome many temptations before the gods finally allow him to reach home and live in peace.

To tell Odysseus's story in this book, we have used both of Homer's great poems. Pages 7–13 are based on the *Iliad*; the rest is based on the *Odyssey*.

HOW TO PRONOUNCE THE GREEK NAMES

This is how the names of Homer's characters are usually pronounced in English. Experts in ancient Greek may pronounce them differently.

Achilles = a-KILL-eez
Agamemnon = ag-a-MEM-non
Aphrodite = aff-rod-EYE-tee
Apollo = a-POLL-oh
Artemis = ART-e-miss
Athena = ath-EE-nah
Calypso = ka-LIP-soe
Charybdis = ka-RIB-diss
Ciconians = sik-OH-nee-ans
Circe = SIR-see
Cyclops = SY-clops (plural:
   Cyclopes = SY-clo-pees)
Hera = HEAR-a

Heracles = HAIR-ah-kleez
Ithaca = ITH-a-ka
Lotus = LOW-tus
Menelaus = men-ell-AY–us
Nausicaa = naw-sic-AY-ah or
   now-sic-AY-ah
Odysseus = odd-ISS-ee-us
Penelope = pen-EL-o-pee
Poseidon = poss-EYE-don
Scylla = SILL-a
Tiresias = tie-REE-see-us
Telemachus = tell-EM-a-kus
Zeus = ZOOS

ODYSSEUS'S VOYAGE HOME

Homer mentions many different places in his two great poems, the *Odyssey* and the *Iliad*. But, in spite of this, we cannot be exactly sure where Odysseus travelled on his long voyage home from Troy. Homer's descriptions of land and sea are dramatic, but he was telling a story, not compiling a travel guide. Some of Homer's names for places are no longer widely used; others have vanished altogether.

Almost certainly, Homer had not visited all the places he mentions; nor had his audience. As Odysseus's adventures make clear, travel was difficult and often dangerous in ancient Greek lands. For readers today, trying to follow Odysseus's wanderings is an interesting challenge, but failure does not matter. Odysseus's journey is first and foremost a voyage of dreams and possibilities; the brave cities and beautiful islands of the *Odyssey* and the *Iliad* belong to a landscape of the imagination that may, or may not, be the same as the real world.

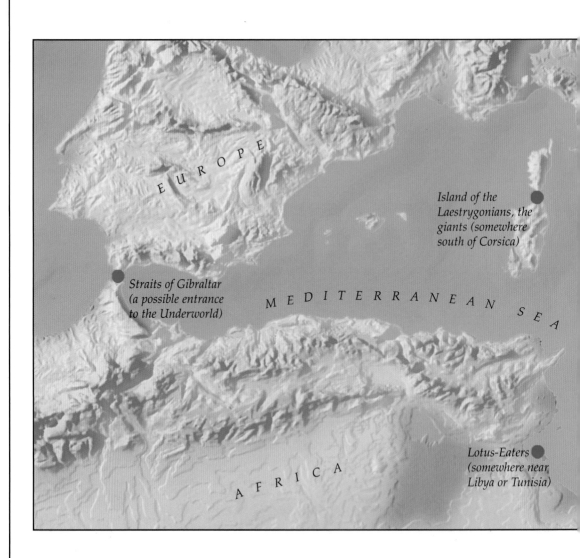

EUROPE

Island of the Laestrygonians, the giants (somewhere south of Corsica)

Straits of Gibraltar (a possible entrance to the Underworld)

MEDITERRANEAN SEA

Lotus-Eaters (somewhere near Libya or Tunisia)

AFRICA

On his journey, Odysseus meets few normal humans, but many witches, magicians, monsters, and gods. They are superhuman, and they call on him to be extraordinary also. Odysseus begins by being bold and cunning; as he travels, he learns patience, wisdom, and respect for the gods. Throughout, he remains tough, hopeful, and, above all, loyal: to his comrades, his homeland, his family—and to himself. He refuses Calypso's offer of everlasting life on her island, because that would mean forgetting his own true identity.

Odysseus's adventures amaze and inspire us. They also make us think. What can we do, what can we achieve, if, like Odysseus, we are brave and clever and daring?

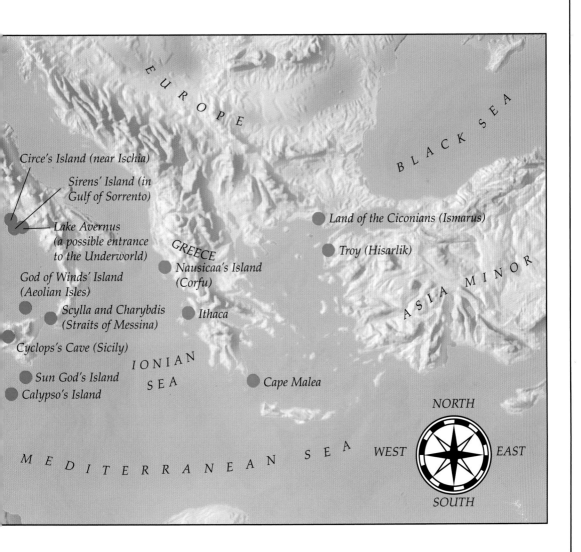

Circe's Island (near Ischia)

Sirens' Island (in Gulf of Sorrento)

Lake Avernus (a possible entrance to the Underworld)

God of Winds' Island (Aeolian Isles)

Scylla and Charybdis (Straits of Messina)

Cyclops's Cave (Sicily)

Sun God's Island

Calypso's Island

EUROPE

BLACK SEA

Land of the Ciconians (Ismarus)

Troy (Hisarlik)

GREECE
Nausicaa's Island (Corfu)

Ithaca

ASIA MINOR

IONIAN SEA

Cape Malea

MEDITERRANEAN SEA

NORTH

WEST   EAST

SOUTH

43

ODYSSEUS AND ARCHEOLOGY

For centuries, people have tried to link the details of Homer's poems with real historical events, especially the Trojan War. They have hoped to find the city where Odysseus, Helen, Paris, Menelaus, and many other characters from Homer's poems lived, loved, and quarrelled. Of course, no one knows whether Odysseus, Helen, or any of Homer's characters ever really existed; they might be completely imaginary, or based on half-forgotten memories of dead noble ancestors and famous warriors.

THE REAL TROY

Mycenae (where Homer said Agamemnon ruled) and Sparta (where Homer said Helen lived) are still in existence today. And the site of the city of Troy has been known since ancient Greek times. It is on the northwest coast of Asia Minor (now Turkey), close to the entrance to the Hellespont—a narrow channel of seawater that links the Mediterranean Sea to the Black Sea. Today, Troy is known in Turkish as Hisarlik; the remains of its past buildings form a *tell* (huge mound) a hundred feet high, with further ruins close by.

The first excavations at Troy began in 1871, and were led by German amateur archeologist Heinrich Schliemann (1822–1890). Schliemann used primitive—and potentially damaging—techniques. But he discovered that the tell at Troy contained the remains of several different cities, built one on top of the other. In one of the lowest, earliest, levels, he found beautiful gold jewellery which he named "King Priam's Treasure," including a crown

which, he thought, might have been worn by Helen of Troy. (We now know that he was wrong: the treasure was fashioned around 2000 B.C., and that is much earlier than the probable date of the Trojan War—see below.)

There have been several other archeological investigations of Troy since Schliemann's time. Today, archeologists think that Troy was first occupied around 3000 B.C., rebuilt several times, then finally deserted by the Trojans soon after 1200 B.C. It was taken over by Greek settlers and rebuilt once again around 800 B.C.

Excavations at Troy have revealed nine main layers of settlement, each one belonging to a different stage in the city's history. Levels VI and VII (from around 1200 B.C.) show that Troy was rich and powerful at that time. It controlled ships sailing between the Mediterranean and the Black Sea, and traded with many neighboring peoples.

WAS THERE A REAL TROJAN WAR?

In Troy layers VI and VII, archeologists have found the ruins of a great citadel (royal fortress) and a massive horseshoe-shaped defensive ditch—together with many skeletons, slingshot stones, and fire-damaged buildings dating from around 1180 B.C. Written records left by the Hittite people of eastern Asia Minor also report political quarrels in the Troy region at around the same time.

Are the finds and the written records evidence for Homer's Trojan War? It seems very likely, but we cannot be completely certain. Archeologists have not yet been able to identify the enemies who destroyed Troy. Probably they were Greeks, as Homer's poems say, but it is just possible that they were invaders from further north, beyond the Black Sea.

For further details, see:
http://www.archaeology.org/0405/etc/troy.html
For computer reconstructions:
http://www.uni-tuebingen.de/troia/vr/vr0207_en.html (Go to "Troy level VI" to see reconstructions of Troy at the probable time of the Trojan War.)

WHO WERE THE TROJANS?

The people who lived in Troy were not Greeks. They did not speak a Greek language or share in Greek civilization, though they did trade with rich and powerful Greek cities, including Mycenae. They had close political and cultural connections with the powerful Hittite empire, based further east in Asia Minor. In their own language, they called their city "Wilusa"; this became "Ilium" in Greek. In his poems, Homer often uses "Ilium" as another name for Troy; that's why his poem about the Trojan War is called the *Iliad*.

Heinrich Schliemann's Greek wife, Sophia, wearing part of the so-called "King Priam's Treasure." This collection of gold jewellery from ancient Troy was actually made long before the likely date of the Trojan War.

ODYSSEUS'S ISLAND

Homer's *Odyssey* tells us that Odysseus's homeland is the kingdom of Ithaca. Today, Ithaca (or Ithaki) is the name of an island in the Ionian Sea, off the coast of western Greece. But readers who visit modern Ithaca are often puzzled by Homer's poem, which describes Ithaca as low-lying, far out to sea, and facing westward. But the island of Ithaca we see today is rather different: mountainous, facing southeast, and sheltered from the open sea by a bigger island, called Kefalonia.

However, in the 1890s, local people on Ithaca unearthed finds of pottery and metalwork—especially a bronze tripod and cauldron—rather like those mentioned in Homer's poems. These finds suggested that a powerful king lived on the island around the probable time of the Trojan War—that is, around 1180 B.C. Then, in 1930, British archeologist Sylvia Benton found 12 more bronze tripods (in Homer's *Odyssey*, a total of 13 tripods are mentioned as gifts to Odysseus), plus a pottery face-mask (a religious offering) dating from around 300 B.C. The mask was inscribed (carved) with the words:

"My prayer to Odysseus." This suggests that the hero Odysseus was worshipped as a god on Ithaca by later Greek people.

In 2007, a team of geologists and historians, led by British buinessman Robert Bittlestone, made a controversial new suggestion: that Homer's "Ithaca" was not modern Ithaca, but a low-lying peninsula, now named Paliki, on the westward (seaward) side of the nearby island of Kefalonia. In Homer's time, Paliki had also been an island, but later rockfalls and landslides, caused by earthquakes, had filled up the seabed between the islands, and "joined" Paliki to Kefalonia. The team also discovered traces of ancient tracks on Paliki, cut off and blocked by earthquakes, and pottery from the probable time of the Trojan War.

In spite of these discoveries, many experts still feel that the bronze tripods and mask found on Ithaca are more important clues to Odysseus's probable home. They suggest that, in Homer's time, Ithaca and Kefalonia were both part of the same kingdom, named Ithaca, ruled by a single king. Possibly, one of these kings was called Odysseus.

BOOKS, PLAYS, AND FILMS

BASED ON HOMER'S *ODYSSEY*

Ever since Homer's works were rediscovered at the end of the 14th century, his characters and their adventures have inspired writers, artists, and musicians. And his word "Odyssey" has come to mean any long, adventurous journey or quest.

The names of Homer's greatest warriors, Achilles (Greek) and Hector (Trojan), are still symbols of heroism and pride. Helen of Troy is still famous for her beauty—and foolishness. In 1590, she inspired one of the most famous lines from any play, ever: "Is this the face that launched a thousand ships?"[1] It was written by English dramatist Christopher Marlowe, in his play *Doctor Faustus*.

In 1641, Odysseus's story was chosen by Italian composer Claudio Monteverdi when he wrote one of the world's first operas, *The Return of Ulysses to His Homeland*.[2] In 1922, Irish writer James Joyce caused a scandal when he published *Ulysses*—a novel telling the story of an epic inner journey through a young man's troubled and excited mind.

Homer's magicians and monsters, especially Circe the enchantress and the man-eating Cyclopes, have also become world-famous. They are glamorous, exciting, scary, weird—and also share some of the most extreme human characteristics, such as violent rage or lust for power. They shock and fascinate us. Today, they feature in many books, comics, and console and computer games.

In contrast, the adventures of Odysseus and the Trojan War have not inspired many films. Perhaps this is because Homer's vivid images cannot be equalled on the big screen.

1955 *Ulysses* (USA)
Traditional Hollywood epic, starring Kirk Douglas as action hero Odysseus.

1968 *2001: A Space Odyssey* (USA)
One of the most famous films about space ever made. Like Homer's Odysseus, the space travellers face a long, risky voyage which most of them will not survive.

1997 *The Odyssey* (UK)
A popular retelling, originally made for TV. An international cast of stars is led by Armand Assante as Odysseus. The film won an Emmy award.

1998 *The Destruction of Troy and the Adventures of Odysseus*
A series of animated films for children, telling the story of the Trojan War in short episodes.

2000 *O Brother, Where Art Thou?* (USA)
Set in the USA, this tells how three escaped convicts, led by George Clooney, face adventure and danger on a long journey as they try to reach home and safety in the city of Ithaca, New York.

2004 *Troy* (USA)
Starring Brad Pitt, this action movie features a huge cast, amazing sets, dramatic battle scenes, and elaborate costumes.

---

1. in other words: Is this beauty the reason why the Greek army set sail and attacked Troy?
2. Ulysses is the Latin form of the name Odysseus.

INDEX